Secrets and Shadows

Kimberly Yohey

ISBN 978-1-0980-9394-5 (paperback)
ISBN 978-1-0980-9395-2 (digital)

Christian Faith Publishing, Inc.
832 Park Avenue
Meadville, PA 16335
www.christianfaithpublishing.com

Printed in the United States of America

Introduction

I NEVER BELIEVED IT WHEN THEY said your life can change in one night, but I do now. I never would have expected my life to go this way, but I would never change anything about it.

Everything that has happened has led me to where I am, surrounded by the people I love.

Life may have thrown some rocky things my way, but in the end, I am still alive and I still have my family. There are so many ways I could have turned out from the things life threw at me, but I am glad I turned out the way I did. It has made me a better person, and I personally think it has made me a better mother to my baby girl. When everything started, I had no idea how it was going to end. There were so many bumpy roads that I had no idea how we were going to get through them, but we did. It made me appreciate my friends and family more. This is the story of the rocky path my life took. It's the secrets I tried to keep, and the shadows he lurked behind.

My Baby Girl

I WOKE UP TO THE SOUND of someone screaming. I got up and ran to Emma's room. She was sitting on her bed, crying. I walked over to her. I sat on the bed and hugged her tightly.

"It's okay, baby. Mommy's here," I said. "I promise I won't ever let anyone hurt you. It was just a dream. Everything is all right."

I pulled her close to me. I laid her down on her bed and pulled her down to lay next to me. I played with her hair until she went to sleep. I stayed with her all night. It has been a long time since I got to sleep through the night. I usually spend my time thinking. My life has been complicated for the past two years. I was dating this guy when I was fifteen years old. One night he told me that if I loved him, I would sleep with him. I thought that he loved me, so that's what I did.

After I did, he left for a trip with his parents and wouldn't talk to me anymore. That changed when I started telling him that I wasn't feeling very well. A few weeks later, I found out that I was pregnant with Emma. After I had her, he wanted to be around. My parents let him stay with us.

He stayed in my room at night because Emma had the spare room. At night we would talk, but if I said anything wrong, then he would beat me. I let it slide for a while, but my parents started to notice. I remember the day my mom found out. It wasn't even because I told her.

Flashback

I'm sitting in a rocking chair in Emma's room. She woke up from her nap and I was trying to get her to go back to sleep. It took a few minutes, but she finally went back to sleep. Tyler walked into the room. He took Emma from my arms and laid her down in her crib. I stood up.

"I'm going to go and try to get some sleep while she is napping," I said.

I went to turn around, but he grabbed my arm.

"I saw you looking at her. I know what you were thinking and you will never take her away from me," he said.

"Tyler, let go of me. You're hurting me," I said.

I looked up and saw my mother standing in the doorway.

"Let go of my daughter. I think you need to leave now, Tyler," my mom said.

Tyler stood up straight and left. My mom yelled after him that he could see Emma as long as we were with him and he didn't hurt me.

*****

Everything was fine after that until Emma was a year old. Tyler wanted to see her more, and when he came over, he started to hit me again. My mom took him to court, and I got sole custody of Emma. Tyler can see her, but he has to call and talk to me about it first. We moved a few weeks ago. My dad got a job offer that he couldn't refuse. He works for a gym company. They were building a new one and the boss wanted my dad to watch over construction and then be in charge of the gym. My dad obviously said yes. We were very happy for him. Tyler knew we were moving, and I had to give him my address. I started at my new school in the morning. My mom didn't work, so she took care of Emma while I was at school. It was after midnight when I finally fell asleep.

I woke up to the sound of my alarm on my phone. I got up. It was six thirty. I had to be at the school by seven thirty. I got up and got dressed. I wore jeans, a T-shirt, and my purple Nike tennis shoes. I grabbed my bag and went downstairs. My mom was sitting at the kitchen table. I sat my bag down on one of the chairs.

"I made coffee. I know you didn't get much sleep last night, so you are gonna need it," she said.

"Thanks, Mom. I don't know what I would do without you," I said.

My mom just laughed. Our relationship had gotten stronger ever since I had Emma. I feel like I finally understand how my mom feels about me since I now have my own daughter. I finished my coffee and got another cup to take with me to school.

"Okay, don't forget, Emma needs to be up by eight and she needs her nap about one. If she sleeps well, let her sleep until I get home. She has been having bad nightmares," I said.

"Honey, I know. She will be okay," she said.

I gave her a hug and went out to my car. I have a Kia Sportage. I also have a car seat in the back for Emma. I drove to the school. I parked my car and went to the office. I heard whistles around me from the guys. Since I had Emma, I had gotten a better figure and I wasn't afraid to show it off. I walked into the office and saw three guys sitting on the only three chairs.

Meet the Bad Boys

THE THREE BOYS LOOKED UP at me. I walked over to the counter and looked at the lady who was sitting behind the desk.

"Hello. What can I do for you today?" the lady asked.

"I'm new. I need to pick up my schedule," I said.

"What's your name dear?" she asked.

"It's Evie Mathews," I said.

"Okay, here you go. Your locker number and its combination is at the top. Let me know how your day goes," she said.

"Thank you," I said.

I turned around and walked out of the office. I saw that the three guys were still staring at me. I looked at my schedule when I was out of the office:

- 1st—English
- 2nd—math
- 3rd—gym
- 4th—history
- 5th—lunch
- 6th—chemistry
- 7th—art

I walked to my locker. I put my bag in my locker. I put my phone in my pocket and went to class. I walked in and saw that the only seat left was by a blond girl. I sat down next to her.

"Hello, my name is Haily. You must be new," she said.

"It's nice to meet you. I'm Evie," I said.

"Well, I'm glad I got to be the first to meet you. You should sit with me at lunch," Haily said.

"Sure, that sounds like fun," I said.

"Just so you're not afraid at lunch. I sit with the three bad boys of the school," she said.

I was shocked at first because she seemed nice and like a good girl, but it's not my place to judge people when I just meet them.

"That's fine," I said.

"Really? You're not judging or anything?" Haily asked.

"No. Why would I judge you when I don't know you that well?" I asked.

She smiled at me.

"Wow. You are the first girl I have met that hasn't judged me," she said.

I frowned. Why would someone judge her just by who she sits with.

"That's a terrible thing for people to do," I said.

She nodded her head in agreement.

When class was over, I went to my next class. I didn't have Haily in any of my other classes so far. My classes went by fast, and it was now lunch. I walked in and saw Haily with the three guys I saw this morning. I sat down next to Haily.

"Hey. I'm glad that you made it," she said.

I smiled. It's nice to have made a friend on the first day. It makes the day easier.

"Me too. Who are your friends?" I asked.

Haily looked up and pointed them out to me.

"That is Dan, Steve, and Derrick," Haily said.

"It's nice to meet all of you," I said.

They just nodded their head once like they didn't care.

"They just aren't too nice to people at first, but once they get to know you, then they don't seem so mean," Haily said.

I smiled and nodded my head. I felt my phone vibrating. It was my mom. I answered right away.

"Hey, Mom, what's up?" I asked.

"Hey, honey. It's nothing. Your dad has to go out of town for a few days, and he needs me to go with him. I took Emma over to the neighbors' house. She said that she could watch Emma until you got home and then tomorrow while you are at school," my mom said.

"Okay. Anything else?" I said.

"Tyler called this morning. He's gonna come see Emma tonight. I hope you are okay with that," she said.

"No, that's fine. I will talk to you later," I said.

"Okay, honey, see you in a few days. Bye," she said.

I said bye and hung up.

"Hey. Is everything okay?" Haily asked.

"Yeah. Everything's fine. She just told me that she and my dad are gonna be out of town for a few days," I said.

She nodded her head. To be honest, I was kind of scared. I have always had my mom and my dad around when Tyler was seeing Emma. I must have zoned out because Derrick threw something at me. I looked up right away.

"What?" I asked.

"Aren't you going to get your lunch?" Derrick asked.

"No. I'm not really hungry," I said.

He just shrugged his shoulders.

After lunch, I went to chemistry class. I sat in the back. I saw Dan walk in. He took a seat next to me. The teacher walked in. We took notes the whole time. About five minutes before the bell rang, he started talking.

"You're gonna be doing a project. The person sitting next to you is your partner. This is an out-of-class project," he said.

Great. My partner is Dan. I looked over at Dan.

"Do you want to come to my house or go to yours?" Dan asked.

"Can we go to my house?" I asked.

Dan nodded. This was my chance to not be alone with Tyler.

"Okay. Is right after school okay with you?" I asked.

He nodded his head again. I wrote down my address and gave it to him. When the bell rang, I went to art class. The art teacher started by giving us a project. It was to draw a picture of the person who means the most to us. I started to draw my Emma. I had just finished with her eyes when the bell rang.

Bad Boy Meets Baby Girl

I STOOD UP AND WALKED TO my locker. I got my bag and went to my car. I drove home. I parked my car in the driveway. I walked over to the neighbors' house. I knocked on the door. A lady answered.

"Hi. My name is Evie. I'm here to pick up Emma," I said.

"It's nice to meet you. I'm Alice. Emma is in on the couch," she said.

She moved and opened the door wider, telling me to come in. I stepped in and saw Emma sitting on the couch. She looked up and saw me. She smiled really big.

"Hi, Mommy," she said.

I laughed. She was so excited to see me, like she always is.

"Hi, baby. Are you ready to go home?" I asked.

She nodded and walked over to me. I looked to Alice.

"Thank you for watching her," I said.

"It's no problem. I can't wait to watch her tomorrow too," she said.

I smiled one more time before I walked back over to my house. I unlocked the door and walked in. I took my jacket off and put my bag on the counter. I got my phone and turned the sound back up.

"Hey, baby, do you want to play outside?" I asked.

She smiled real big and nodded. I opened the door and stepped onto the porch. I was only wearing my T-shirt, so I could see the tattoo on the inside of my arm by my wrist. Emma saw a feather one day and loved it so much, so I drew a picture of one. She loved it so much, so I got it tattooed to my arm. She was so happy when she saw it. I was watching her when a car pulled into the driveway, followed by another car. This one I knew right away. It was Tyler's car. He was the second car. The other car I didn't know until he got out. It was Dan. Tyler went to walk over to Emma, but she ran over to me. He looked really mad. Dan, however, just walked right up to me.

Emma kind of stumbled on the stairs and he straightened her out.

"Thank you," I said.

"No problem," he said.

Tyler reached us. He looked down to Emma, who was clutching onto my leg.

"Hey, Emma, don't you want to give me a hug?" he asked.

Emma shook her head no.

"Why not?" he asked.

He sounded hurt, but his face said that it just made him mad.

"No hurt, Mommy," she said.

"I'm not gonna hurt, Mommy," Tyler said.

She gave him a knowing look. She was waiting for him to hurt me. I hated that when she was around her dad, she was worried about him hurting me. I wanted her to be okay around her dad, but after everything he has done, I know that is going to be impossible.

"Emma. You know you have to spend a little time with him. Why don't you show him the flowers that you helped me plant yesterday?" I said.

She nodded. I moved my arm and Tyler saw my tattoo. He grabbed my arm, but I jerked it away from him as fast as I could.

"Why do you have a tattoo? You know what I said about them," Tyler said.

"Yes, I know what you said, but I don't care," I said.

He looked back at Emma. She was watching him carefully. He got an evil look and walked over to her. I watched as she walked to the garden. I turned to Dan.

"I'm sorry. I didn't think he would be here this soon," I said.

"It's fine. She's your daughter, isn't she?" he asked.

I nodded my head.

"Why didn't you tell me? I never would have brought up going to my house if I knew," he said.

"I didn't want you to judge me," I said.

I looked up at him. I heard a cry and then looked over to Emma. She was on the ground. Tyler was just standing there not doing anything. She was holding her ankle and crying. I walked over to her. Dan was behind me.

"Baby girl, what happened?" I asked.

She looked up to Tyler. I looked over at him and he had his evil smile.

"I think you have seen her enough for today. You should go," I said.

"Fine. I will see you tomorrow," Tyler said.

"No you won't," I said.

Tyler walked over to me and yanked me up and away from Emma. He was gripping my arm tightly.

"Listen, you will not keep me from seeing my own daughter," he said.

"Why? The way you keep going here, soon you won't be able to see her anymore. If you keep hurting her, then she won't want to see you, and it will be your own fault," I said.

He let go of my arm and slapped me. I fell to the ground. I saw Dan grab Tyler's shirt.

"You need to leave now," Dan said.

His voice was low, and he sounded so threatening. I saw Tyler clench his jaw, but he decided to listen to Dan. Dan let go of his shirt.

Hospital

I LOOKED AT DAN. TYLER NODDED his head and left. I got to my knees and crawled over to Emma. I wanted to make sure she was all right.

"Are you okay, baby?" I asked.

She shook her head. I looked over to Dan.

"Can you drive us to the hospital?" I asked.

"Yes. Of course," Dan said.

I picked Emma up carefully. Alice stepped outside. She looked over at us, and her face was full of worry. I walked over to Dan's car. He opened the door for me and I got in. I held Emma, and she was crying.

"It's gonna be okay, baby. When grandpa gets back, we will talk to him about making sure he won't hurt us ever again, okay?" I said.

She nodded her head.

We got to the hospital. I walked in with Dan behind me. I walked up to the desk.

"May I help you?" the lady said.

"Yes, I think my daughter hurt her ankle," I said.

The lady looked at Emma.

"Okay, I'm just gonna take her to the back. Can you wait out here please?" the lady said.

I was confused but nodded my head anyway. A minute later, she came back.

"Do you know what happened?" she asked me.

"She was in the yard playing with her dad, and the next thing I know I hear her scream, and when I looked, she was holding her ankle crying," I said.

The look on the lady's face said that she thought that I was not telling the truth. It made me mad.

"Do you honestly think that I would hurt my own baby girl?" I asked.

"I have seen it before," the lady said.

"I didn't hurt my baby girl," I said.

She looked at me and nodded her head. I walked over to the chairs and sat down. I wasn't paying attention. I couldn't believe that I let him hurt my baby. I looked up real fast when Dan bumped my arm. I saw a doctor standing there. I stood up really fast.

"Are you Emma's parents?" the doctor asked.

"I'm her mom. Is she okay?" I asked him.

"Yes, she is fine. She just sprained her ankle a little bit, but it will be ok. It might hurt for a few weeks, but that's normal," he said.

I nodded my head. I was relieved that she was okay and it wasn't anything serious.

"Can I see her?" I asked.

The doctor nodded his head.

"Yeah. I will be right in with her papers, and then you can go home," he said.

"Okay, thank you," I said.

I walked back to the room where I saw the lady at the desk take her to. She was sitting on the bed and her ankle was wrapped. I walked over and I hugged her. I could feel my tears starting to fall. I pulled away from her and she looked at me.

"Why Mommy sad?" Emma asked.

I gave a fake smile so I could try to keep her from worrying about me.

"Mommy's not sad, baby. I'm happy," I said.

"Why cry?" she asked.

"Happy tears. I'm happy that my baby is okay," I said.

The doctor walked in. He gave me her papers and then we left. Once in the car, I heard my phone going off. It was my mom. I wiped my tears and answered.

"Hey, Mom," I said.

"Honey, what's the matter? You sound like you have been crying," she said.

"Tyler was over. Mom, he hurt Emma. We are on our way home from the hospital," I said.

"The hospital? Is she okay? How bad is she hurt?" she asked.

"She's fine. She just has a sprained ankle," I said.

"Okay, that's it, we are coming back home," she said.

"No, it's okay. We will be fine for one night. I made a friend at school. I will just ask if they will stay the night with me," I said.

"Okay, honey. Let me know if anything else happens, okay?" she said.

I told her I would, and then we hung up. I looked over at Dan.

"Do you think Haily would stay the night with me?" I asked.

"I'll stay with you. My parents don't care what I do or where I'm at," Dan said.

"Thank you so much for everything you have done for me today," I said.

The rest of the car ride was quiet. When we pulled up, I got Emma out of the back seat. I walked to the door. I had my keys in my hand. Dan took them from me and opened the door for me. I walked in and took Emma upstairs. I put her on her bed and kissed her forehead. I walked back downstairs. Dan was at the kitchen table.

"She sleeping?" Dan asked.

"Yeah. I can't thank you enough for this. I don't know many people that would have helped me like you did," I said.

"It's not a problem. I just did what I thought was right," he said.

Dan was different from others I met. He was nice and didn't push about Emma. Most people, when they found out I had a daughter, would automatically ask me if I was raped—but I wasn't. I just didn't know that Tyler is the way that he is.

"Can I ask you something?" Dan asked.

I nodded my head.

"How many times has that guy hurt Emma before?" Dan asked.

"That's the first time that he has ever hurt her. Normally, he just hits me or pushes me around, but you were here, so he thought he wouldn't be able to do that this time. I should have known he was going to do something. It was all over his face. I can't believe I turned around and took my eyes off of her. It's my fault. I'm supposed to protect her and I didn't do that," I said.

Dan hugged me to him. I hugged him back. He rubbed the back of my shoulder.

"Why does he hurt you?" Dan asked.

"He says that I ruined his life because I got pregnant," I said.

"That's ridiculous. He should have been happy that you had Emma," Dan said.

"He wasn't always like this. I had Emma a month after I turned fifteen. When she was first born, he was really sweet. Even while I was pregnant, he was so sweet. He helped me with everything.

"After Emma was a few months old, he started to beat me. He would call me names, said that since Emma cried a lot, that I was a bad mom. A year after that, my mom saw that he was about to hit me one day. The worst part was that he was gonna hit me because I wanted to go lay down. Isn't that stupid?" I said. "Anyway, she made him leave. I got sole custody of her. He can see her, but someone has to watch him. A few weeks ago, we moved here because my dad got a good job offer. I didn't want to give him my address, but the court said that I had to. I have never felt so helpless until today. Today I felt like there was nothing that I could do to protect my little girl," I said.

"You did protect her though. It's not as bad as what it could have been. She's still here," Dan said.

"This time, yeah, but what about next time? You heard him say that he wanted to see her tomorrow. What if he kidnaps her or hurts her or worse? She's only two. A two-year-old shouldn't have to go through that," I said.

Dan looked at me. He looked like he was thinking about something.

"How about every time he comes over, you text me and I will sit with you so you can make sure that nothing happens to her?" Dan asked.

"Why would you do that for me?" I asked him.

"I don't know. I just feel like I need to protect you and her," Dan said.

I smiled at him. I know that I don't know him, but his kindness is greatly appreciated.

"Thank you," I said.

Dan nodded his head once.

Getting Started

WE WERE STILL IN THE kitchen. I knew there was a good chance that neither of us were going to get very much sleep.

"We should get started on our project," I said.

"Yeah, that's a good idea," Dan said.

"Oh, and by the way, in advance, I want to say that I'm sorry. There is a very high chance that we won't get any sleep," I said.

He looked confused but nodded his head.

A few hours later, we were working on our project. It was almost midnight. I know this is usually the time that the nightmares start. I was in the middle of writing the notes when I heard it start. Emma started to scream, but it was different this time. I heard a bang upstairs. I stood up so fast that the chair I was on fell over and crashed onto the floor. I took the steps two at a time. I got to Emma's room.

She was on her bed crying hysterically. I went to walk over to her but stepped on glass. I looked down and her window had been smashed by a brick. I picked it up and looked at it. There was a note on it.

> *Don't think that you will ever take her from me. I will kill you before you can even try to think about it.*
>
> *—T*

I put the brick down. I didn't care that the glass was cutting into the bottoms of my feet. I went over to the bed and picked Emma up. I walked back over the glass and left her room. I walked back to the kitchen and sat on a different chair. I sat Emma on the table. I grabbed my phone and called 911. While the phone was ringing, I was checking her for any signs of injury. I didn't see any, thankfully.

"Nine-one-one. What is your emergency?" the dispatcher asked.

"I need the police to come to my house. Someone threw a brick through my daughter's bedroom window," I said.

"Okay, where do you live?" she asked.

I gave her my address and she said that the police would be there soon and left it on emergency, so if anything else happened, I could just press the button and it would alert her.

It was only a few minutes before the cops showed up.

"Hello, ma'am. My name is Officer Jones. Can you tell me what happened?" the officer said.

"I was down here working on my chemistry project for school. I know my daughter gets nightmares and I was listening for her scream, but when she screamed it sounded different, and I heard a bang. I got up the stairs as fast as possible and found the window broken and a brick on the ground. I picked it up to look at it and saw a note on it. It's still upstairs," I said.

"Do you mind if I go up and look?" the officer asked.

"No, go right ahead," I said.

He walked up the stairs. Dan looked over at me. I could see that he was silently asking me if I was okay. I just looked away from him. I didn't mean to drag him into the middle of all this. The officer came down and set the brick on the table. I saw Dan lean over and read the piece of paper attached to the brick.

"Do you have any idea who T could be?" the officer asked.

"My ex-boyfriend. His name is Tyler Reid," I said.

"Is he Emma's father?' the officer asked.

I nodded my head.

"Why does he think that you are trying to take her away from him.?" the officer asked.

"He was here earlier to see her and he pushed her down. He made her sprain her ankle," I said.

He looked at my baby girl sitting on the table.

"Do you think that he would follow through with his threat?" the officer asked.

I looked down at the ground. I know how Tyler is.

"I know he will. He would do it in a heartbeat if he thought that he could get away with it," I said.

The officer nodded his head.

"Do you have anywhere to stay?" he asked.

"No, we just moved here and my parents are out of town," I said.

"She can stay with me until her parents come back," Dan said.

I looked over at him.

"Or I can stay here," he added.

"Okay. You two can figure it out. I will make a report and send it to a judge in the morning to see what he wants to do about this situation," the officer said.

I nodded my head. He turned and walked out of the house. I went to put my feet down and remembered that I walked over glass. I hissed in pain. Dan looked over at me quickly.

"What's wrong? Are you okay?" he asked.

"I'm fine. I just hurt my feet on the glass trying to get to my baby girl," I said.

"Where is your first-aid kit?" he asked.

"Upstairs in the medicine cabinet, above the sink in the bathroom," I said. Dan got up and walked upstairs. I looked at Emma. I was trying not to fall apart in front of my baby. I felt a tear fall. Emma's little hand reached out and wiped it off my cheek.

"Is mommy okay?" Emma asked.

I nodded my head and tried to smile for her.

"Mommy's okay, baby. Are you okay? Did any of the glass hit you when the window broke?" I said.

"No, Mommy. I is okay," she said.

"That's good. Mommy can't have her baby getting hurt," I said.

I saw Dan walk down the stairs. He came over to me.

"Put your feet up on the chair," he said.

I did as I was told. I wasn't prepared when he touched the alcohol to my foot. I hissed in pain. Emma looked at Dan.

"No hurt Mommy," she said to him.

"I'm not hurting your mommy, I promise. The medicine just burns a little, but that's okay. It means that it's helping her," Dan said.

She looked at him. I could tell she wasn't sure if she should believe him or not.

"Okay, I trust you," she said.

I looked at Dan. He looked up and we locked eyes. I smiled. No one has ever done that before. Once he was finished, he wrapped my feet in gauze. He picked my feet up and sat on the chair with my feet on his lap. I went to put my feet down, but he put his hand on my leg to tell me to keep them there. I looked at Emma. I could see she was getting tired. She crawled from the table to my lap. I hugged her close to me. It was only a few minutes before I heard her breathing slow down and knew that she was asleep. I looked over at Dan. My phone started ringing. Dan picked it up and handed it to me. I saw that it was my mom. I answered it.

The Call

I ANSWERED MY PHONE. I DIDN'T want her to worry, but I knew she has to know.

"Hey, Mom," I said.

"Hey, baby. Did Emma have a nightmare again?" she asked.

"Sort of. It was also kind of a real-life nightmare," I said.

"Why, honey? What happened?" she asked.

I knew the tone of her voice would catch my dad. I heard the phone switch hands.

"Sweetie, what happened?" my dad asked.

"It's Tyler. He threw a brick through Emma's window. He taped a note to it. He said if I even try to think about taking her from him, then he will kill me," I said.

I realized I was crying again.

"We will be there in the morning, okay, baby?" my dad said. "How are you holding up?"

"I'm scared, Daddy," I said.

"Oh, baby. I wish we could get there sooner," he said.

"I know. It's okay. You didn't know that this was going to happen," I said.

I wiped my cheeks.

"Are you in the house by yourself?" he asked.

"No. A brave friend from school is staying with me. He has helped a lot today. He even made Emma feel better when she thought that he was hurting me," I said.

"Why did she think that?" he asked.

"To get to her on her bed, I had to walk on glass and he cleaned my feet up but forgot to warn me about the alcohol, and I made a noise and she yelled at him and told him not to hurt her mommy. He told her that it was supposed to sting 'cause that meant it was helping," I said.

"He sounds like a wonderful young man," my dad said.

"Wow. That's a first. You haven't even met him and you already like him better than Tyler," I said.

I looked up at Dan and he smiled at me.

"That's because he is helping my girls and not hurting them," he said.

I smiled and shook my head, even though I knew he couldn't see me.

"I guess that's a good reason," I said.

"I got to go and get some sleep so we can be there in the morning. I love you," he said.

"I love you too," I said.

I hung up the phone. I looked at Dan. He smiled at me.

"Your dad likes me, huh?" he said.

"Yeah. He has a good reason though. He said he likes you because you are helping his girls instead of hurting them," I said.

"What if I told him that I actually like one of his girls?" he asked.

"I don't know. I guess he would like you a lot better than Tyler," I said.

Dan looked at me.

"I am most certain he would like me a lot better than him," Dan said.

I smiled again. I think my dad would like anyone better than Tyler.

Morning

ME AND DAN STAYED IN the same position all night. I finally dozed off at some point. I woke up when I heard the door open. I jumped, but then Dan put his hand on my leg. He looked really tired. I looked behind him and saw my parents. My mom ran to me.

"Oh, my baby girls. I was so worried about you girls," she said.

She was crying on my shoulder. I hugged her as tight as I could while holding Emma.

"I'm okay, Mom. Dan stayed with me all night. He never left us," I said.

She turned to him and hugged him tight.

"Thank you, thank you, thank you so much," she said.

"It's not a problem, I promise. It was nice to hang out with Evie and Emma all night," Dan said.

I looked at the time.

"I have to get ready for school," I said.

My mom took Emma and I got up. Dan stood up too. I walked with him to the door.

"I'm gonna go home and change. I will be right back to give you a ride to school," he said.

"You don't have to do that," I said.

"Yes, I do. If you drive, your feet are just gonna hurt worse. I will be back," he said.

He leaned down and kissed my cheek and then walked out. I stood at the door watching him.

When he left, I went upstairs to my room. I put on black leggings, a black T-shirt, and black boots.

I didn't bother to get my jacket because it was warm outside. I grabbed my bag and went downstairs. I put my bag on the back of the couch and went to the kitchen. I put coffee in my travel mug and grabbed a bowl of cereal. I ate it really fast before Dan got back. I saw him pull into the driveway again.

"I will see you guys after school, okay?" I said.

They both nodded. I kissed my mom on the cheek and went out the door. I went out and got in Dan's car.

"Haily is going to flip when she sees us pull in," he said laughing.

"Why? Does she like you? You know it's not very nice to make a girl jealous," I said.

Dan laughed, but I was being completely serious.

"No, she doesn't like me. I just never let anyone get in my car, let alone stay with them the whole night," he said.

"Why? Did you?" I asked.

"You looked so scared. I didn't want to leave until I knew that you were safe. That, and you're different. You're not like other girls. You're special," he said.

I smiled and looked down.

"I'm special, huh?" I said.

He took a glance at me and chuckled.

"You have no idea how special you are," he said.

"Well, maybe one day I will find someone who will tell me how special I am," I said.

He pulled into a parking spot. He looked over at me.

"You're too special. No one would ever be able to put it into words. No matter how hard they tried, it would never work," he said.

I blushed and looked down. He went to kiss my cheek when I saw a girl running over to the car and noticed it was Haily. I giggled and grabbed my bag. I opened the door and got out. Dan got out of the car too. Haily looked at us and smiled.

"Wow, she must be a special person. You never let anyone ride in your car," she said.

I looked down blushing again, thinking about what he had just said. We walked inside.

Fight

I WALKED OUT OF MY LAST class. I know I have to wait for Dan because he is the one who brought me to school this morning. I walked to my locker, but I heard a commotion. I walked the halls trying to find where the noise was coming from. I finally got to the main hallway and saw that there was a fight. I was about to walk away, but then I noticed one of the people in the fight.

I walked closer and shook my head. Dan was fighting some random person. It was only a few seconds before the fight was broken up. I looked at Dan, and I saw him look at me. I turned around and started walking away.

"Evie, wait!" Dan yelled.

I ignored him and kept walking. He knew about everything that happened last night, so I had no idea why he would think that I would wait for him after seeing him in a fight. The last thing I wanted around Emma or myself is another person who is going to remind me of Tyler. I started walking toward my house. I knew I could call my mom, but she was with Emma, and I didn't want to bother the two of them just in case Emma was sleeping.

I was a few blocks away from my house when a car pulled up beside me. My feet were killing me from last night. I looked over and recognized the car to be Dan's. I looked back and just kept walking. I heard him roll the window down.

"Come on, Evie, just get in the car," he said.

"I'm not getting in the car with you," I said.

"I'll just follow you to your house then," he said.

I sighed and stopped walking. I turned and looked at him. I raised an eyebrow and waited for him to start talking.

"I know you don't want another person like your ex, but I promise I had a good reason back there with that guy," he said.

"There is never a good reason to beat someone like that," I said. "Have you ever been on the receiving end of that?"

He looked at me closely. I saw him close his eyes for a second before he opened them and looked back at me.

"No, I haven't," he said.

"Maybe you should think about that the next time," I said.

"You could explain it to me so I understand it better," he said.

"Fine," I said.

I walked over and got into the car with him. I put my seatbelt on and he started driving. He glanced over at me.

"Do you honestly want to know?" I asked.

"Of course," he said.

"When you are on the receiving end of something like that, all you feel is helpless," I said. "You can only hope that the person will stop before they kill you. Or you can hope that they will kill you quickly instead of slowly."

"I didn't know that," he said.

"It's a terrible feeling that you never get past," I said.

"I'm sorry. I didn't know," he said.

"It gives you something to think about the next time," I said.

He nodded but continued driving. I could tell that he was actually taking in my words. To him, they might not mean much, but it did give him something to think about the next time he finds himself close to a fight.

"Can I ask why you were in that fight to begin with?" I asked.

"He was making comments about Haily in class, and they made her uncomfortable," he said.

"So you did it to defend her?" I said.

He nodded again. I could understand his reasoning. Defending someone is a good reason, but I would still never do that to a person. I knew he just wanted to protect his friends, but there are some things that you just can't do. I would understand more if it was just a hit or two, but to repeatedly hit someone for that reason would be too much. They either learn the lesson after a few hits, or they aren't going to learn it at all.

I Like You a Lot

A month later

A LOT HAS HAPPENED IN THE past month. I turned eighteen. Emma's birthday is in a few weeks. She is super excited to be turning three. Tyler is no longer a problem. A judge called me the next day after the incident and talked to me. After a few questions, he said that I now have a restraining order and Tyler has to do a few years in jail. He also said that if Tyler contacts me before Emma is eighteen, then he can be arrested again. I woke up to my alarm. I got dressed for school. I put on jean cutoff shorts that were cut off at just above mid-thigh. I also had a tank top and cowboy boots. I grabbed my bag and went downstairs. I put my bag on the back of the couch. I went to the kitchen. I got a bowl of cereal. I waited until I saw a car pull into the driveway before I grabbed my bag and left. My mom and dad were still asleep. Once I was outside, I turned and locked the door. I thought it was Haily, but it was Dan's car. I haven't seen him for a few days. I got in the car.

"Hey," I said.

"Hey, did you miss me?" he asked.

I shrugged my shoulders. He laughed and kissed my cheek. We have gotten a lot closer in the past month.

"Is your dad gonna be home tonight?" he asked.

"No, he has to be at the gym until eight. Why?" I said.

"I just want to ask him something," he said.

I raised an eyebrow at him, but he just shrugged. He turned the radio on and Chris Lane's "Fix" was playing on the radio. We listened to it all the way to school. We turned in our project last week and got an A, but we still hung out after school. He pulled into a parking spot and we got out.

Steve and Derrick were watching us. Dan grabbed my hand and laced our fingers. I looked up at him and he just shrugged again. We walked over to Steve, Derrick, and Haily. I sat down next to Haily, but Dan's hand never left my hand.

"I love your outfit. It looks so pretty on you," Haily said.

"Thanks, I actually got to pick this one on my own," I said.

We both laughed. Most nights, Emma helps me pick out an outfit before we go to bed. We heard the bell ring and we all went to class.

At lunch, me and Haily got to the table first. I was going to ask her about Dan, but the boys walked in a few minutes later.

"Do you want to come to my house and hang out after school? Just us girls," I asked her.

"Yes. It will be so much fun. I will drive you home and then we can watch movies with Emma and maybe make cupcakes," Haily said.

I laughed. I told them all about Emma. When they met her, they all loved her. I was happy to actually have friends. Dan sat down next to me.

"I hear that you don't need a ride home now," he said.

I shook my head.

"You know I do have my own car, right?" I asked.

"Yeah, but it's better if I drive you," he said.

"I think it's about the same if I drive myself," I said.

He shook his head.

"Just agree to disagree because he won't change his mind no matter what you say," Steve said.

I knew he was right. So I just shrugged my shoulders.

"At least I won't have to listen to him on the way home," I said, smiling.

"Why? What does he do on the way home?" Haily asked.

"Are you kidding? He never shuts up. He talks about everything," I said.

"I do not talk about everything," Dan said.

"You kind of do. But that's okay," I said, smiling.

"Awww. You guys should get together. You would be so cute," Haily said.

I looked at her and smiled. We both started laughing. Dan looked at us like we were crazy. We kind of were, but it was a good kind of crazy.

After lunch, I went to my classes. My favorite class was art. My art teacher saw my project and said that the girl I drew was very pretty. I couldn't help but smile. I knew my baby girl was pretty, but it was still a good thing to hear from someone else. At the end of the day, I went to my locker and got my bag. I walked out to Haily's car. She and Dan were waiting on me. Haily smiled and then got into her car. I went to open the door, but Dan stopped me.

"I will see you later, okay?" Dan said.

"Of course. I know Emma will be happy to see you," I said.

He smiled and gave me a quick kiss on the lips. After that, he walked away. I stood there, shocked for a second. He usually only kissed me on the cheek. I snapped out of it and got into the car. Haily's mouth was hanging open. I hit her arm.

"Right, sorry," she said.

She started driving to my house.

"You know he has never done that with anyone else before," she added.

I looked at her, shocked. Soon after, we pulled into my driveway. We walked into the house and up the stairs to my room. We put our stuff down and went to Emma's room. I looked in and she was sleeping. I walked over to her and shook her just a little bit. She opened her eyes and looked at me.

"Mommy, you home," she said.

I giggled at her and gave her a hug. I picked her up and we walked downstairs to the living room.

"Haily is going to hang out with us and watch movies," I said. "Is that okay?"

She nodded her head. I laughed at her again. I set her down on the couch and went to get the movies that I know she likes. I brought them to the living room. I laid them out and she picked one. She picked *Cinderella.* It was my favorite one too. I sat next to Emma and Haily sat on the other side of her, and we watched the movie.

Does He Love Me?

I LOOKED OVER AT HAILY. I know this is probably going to be my only chance to ask her about Dan.

"Can I ask you something?" I asked.

She nodded her head.

"How will I know if Dan likes me?" I asked.

She looked at me.

"I don't know. You would have to ask him how he feels," she said. "Do you like him?"

"I'm not sure. I know when he is around, I smile more and he makes me feel safer," I said.

"Oh, you like him," she said.

We both laughed.

"Why did he tell you that he would see you later?" she asked.

I shrugged my shoulders. I really had no idea why he said that. I looked over at Emma.

"Emma, sweetie, what would you like for your birthday?" I asked.

She looked back at me and smiled. I could see that she was thinking.

"I want Mommy," she said.

"I'm here every day, baby," I said.

She thought for a second again.

"Weddy bear," she said.

"A weedy bear?" Haily asked.

I laughed at her.

"She means a teddy bear," I said.

"That's not what it sounded like," Haily said.

"She is only going to be three. She's not good with her words yet," I said.

Haily shrugged and laughed at Emma. I looked at my little girl. She laid down on the floor. By the end of the movie, Emma had fallen asleep on the floor. I got up and picked her up. I set her on the couch and put a blanket over her. I looked over at Haily.

"So do you want to make cupcakes or no?" I asked.

Haily smiled and nodded. I think she is more excited for cupcakes than Emma is. We walked to the kitchen. I got out a cake mix.

Thirty-five minutes later, we were in the kitchen having an icing debate.

"Come on, they are cupcakes. You have to have chocolate icing," Haily said.

I shook my head.

"No way. You need vanilla. They are chocolate cupcakes. That would be too much chocolate on one cupcake," I said.

Haily gasped.

"There is no such thing as having too much. Just use the chocolate icing," she said.

There was a knock on the door.

"Do not touch them," I said.

Haily smiled at me innocently. I shook my head and then walked to the door. Dan was standing there.

"Hey, do you want to come in?" I asked.

"Sure," he said.

I stepped away from the door and let him walk in. I walked back to the kitchen and saw Haily icing the cupcakes.

"Before you freak out, I have a great idea," she said.

"What is your great idea?" I asked.

"We put chocolate icing on half and vanilla on the other half," she said.

I thought about it.

"Fine. I guess that's a good idea," I said.

She smiled at me.

"So what's up, Dan? I didn't expect to see you here at Evie's house," Haily said.

Dan just shrugged his shoulders.

"Come on, you got to give me something. I need details here," she said.

I laughed at her. She sent me a glare. It was supposed to make me stop laughing, but it only made me laugh even harder. I heard a little yawn. It was only a few seconds later when Emma walked in. I looked at her and she walked over to Dan and hugged his leg because that was the only thing she could reach. Dan bent down and picked her up.

"Hey, Emma. How are you?" he said.

"Good. My birfday in a few meeks," she said.

"Weeks, honey, not meeks. Birthday, not birfday," I said.

"And yet you let her say weedy bear," Haily said.

I hit her arm playfully, but she faked being hurt. Emma laughed at the two of us. I looked over at her and smiled.

"You two are so weird," Dan said.

I laughed again. We heard a noise. I looked over at Haily. She checked her phone.

"Sorry, guys, but I got to go," she said.

I nodded my head and said bye as she walked out the door. Dan looked at me.

"So did you talk to my dad yet about whatever it is you wanted him for?" I asked.

Dan chuckled.

"Yes, I talked to him. We had a pleasant conversation," he said.

"That's it. That's all you are going to tell me?" I said.

"Yes, that's all I'm going to tell you," he said.

I shrugged my shoulders. I went to the fridge to find something to cook for dinner. My mom was with my dad at the gym. She doesn't like the idea of him being there alone, so she stayed with him. I couldn't find anything, so I decided to make pasta. I put a pot of water on the stove to boil.

Twenty minutes later, the pasta was done. I put it in bowls to give everyone some, but Dan insisted that he didn't want anything. I sat and ate my food and watched Emma. For a minute, she just played with her food. She went to take a bite but stopped.

"Baby, what's wrong?" I asked her.

She shook her head at me.

"Is it because Grandma and Grandpa aren't here?" I asked.

She nodded her head.

"You know they would want you to eat. You can't become a pretty girl like your mommy if you don't eat," Dan said.

Emma looked up at me and started eating right away. I looked over at Dan. He was staring right back at me.

Once we finished our food, I told Emma that she could watch TV. She quickly went to the living room. I turned to Dan.

"Why did you say that to her?" I asked.

"I'm sorry if I stepped over the line or anything. I really didn't mean to," he said.

"No, it's fine. I was meaning the whole thing about her being pretty like her mommy," I said.

"Oh," he said.

I looked at him, waiting for him to continue, but he never did. I turned around and put the dishes in the sink. I went to start the dishes when he talked.

"What would you say if I told you that I talked to your dad about us?" he asked.

"What do you mean by us? We're just friends, right?" I asked.

"Yeah, we are, but what if I talked to him to see if it was okay about us being more than just friends?" he said.

"Oh," I said.

It was all I said. I didn't know what else to say. What do you say to a person when they say something like that? I was completely shocked.

Confessing

HE WAS WATCHING ME CLOSELY. I could tell that he didn't want to make me feel uncomfortable.

"It's okay if you don't want to talk about that. I was just asking what you thought," Dan said.

"It's fine. I just didn't think that you thought something like that," I said.

I sounded so stupid saying that. I felt like I was only making things even more awkward.

"Why would you think that?" he asks.

I look down at my hands. I thought the answer to that was pretty obvious.

"Come on, I have a baby with a guy who is a big jerk," I said. "Why would you like me?"

He looked at me and shook his head.

"Don't you remember what I told you before?" Dan asked.

I nodded my head. He said that I was special. I was so special that no one would be able to put it into words.

"Then why would you think that I wouldn't like you?" Dan asked.

"You are the only one that said I was special," I said.

"Because I'm right. You are special. So what do you think about there being an us?" Dan said.

I looked at him. The idea was a really good one. Being with him would be a good thing, but I didn't know how Emma would feel, and I didn't know what Tyler would do if he found out I was with someone else.

"I think it would be nice, but I want to talk to Emma about it first and see how she feels," I said.

He nodded his head.

"Okay. Let me know when you decide. I got to go," he said.

I nodded my head. He stood up and gave me a hug before he left. Emma came in from the living room.

"Why did Wan leave?" Emma asked.

"His name is Dan, honey. He had to go somewhere," I said.

I walked over to her and picked her up. I walked back to the living room with her. I sat on the couch with her on my lap.

"I want to ask you something," I said.

She nodded her head and looked at me.

"How would you feel if Dan was over here a lot more often and hung out with me?" I asked.

She looked at me and smiled.

"Great. He nice," she said.

I looked at her. I waited to see if she would say anything else.

"Okay then. I will tell him that," I said.

She hopped down off my lap. I got my phone out and texted Dan.

I talked to Emma. She said great and that you are nice. -E

I waited for about a minute when my phone went off. I looked at the text from Dan.

That's great. So is that a yes to there being an us? -D

I thought for a minute and then replied.

Yes. It's a yes to there being an us. -E

That's awesome. I'm sure Haily will be thrilled to hear that. -D

I just laughed. I'm sure she will be too. Haily was always looking at me and Dan like she was just waiting for us to get together.

I watched Emma sit on the floor playing with dolls. There was a knock at the door. I got up and went to the door. I opened it and saw Tyler. I went to shut it, but he pushed the door open. I turned to Emma.

"Go get Alice, Emma," I yelled.

She got up and ran next door.

"What are you doing here Tyler?" I asked.

"I told you that I would kill you before you took her from me," he said.

Before I registered what he said, I saw a knife. He stretched his arm out and stabbed me in the stomach. He took it out and went to his car and drove off. I stepped onto the porch. I saw Alice running over to me. I went down to my knees. I could hear that she was on the phone. I couldn't understand what she was saying. I looked up at her.

"Is Emma safe?" I asked.

I saw her nod her head. I was starting to feel tired. I closed my eyes. I felt her shake me, but I didn't open my eyes. I heard sirens, but they sounded too far away. I was just hoping that Alice was right when she said that Emma was safe. I would hate it if she was somewhere not safe. I was glad that she didn't see what Tyler did to me. I was so happy that I told her to go get Alice.

Her: Dan's POV

I JUST LEFT EVIE'S HOUSE. THERE was going to be a fight tonight. Me and the boys are gonna go watch it. We had just pulled in when I got a text from Evie. I looked down and checked it.

I talked to Emma and she said great and that you are nice. -E

I read it over a few times before I responded to her.

That's great. So does that mean a yes to there being an us? -D

Yes. That is a yes about there being an us. -E

That's great. I'm sure Haily will be thrilled. -D

I chuckled once I sent it. The boys looked over at me and gave me a weird look.

"I'm texting Evie," I told them.

"I should have known," Steve said.

I hit his arm playfully. Us three were really close, so we knew when we were playing or not. The fight was about to start when my phone rang. It was Evie.

"Hey, what's up?" I said.

"Is this Dan?" some girl asked.

"Yes. Who is this?" I asked.

"This is Alice. I'm Evie's neighbor. I have Emma. The ambulance just left with Evie. I had to call them and Emma insisted that I called you. I have already contacted her parents," she said.

"Is she okay? What happened?" I asked.

"I'm not sure. I just saw a guy leave her house and she was bleeding, so I just called 911," she said.

I told her thanks and then hung up the phone.

"Dude, what's wrong?" Derrick asked.

"I have to go," I said.

I walked away from them. I got to my car and drove to the hospital as fast as I could.

I walked in and went to the desk right away.

"I'm looking for my friend. Her name is Evie," I said.

"Are you family?" the lady asked me.

I shook my head no.

"I'm sorry. I can't give you any information about her status," she said.

I heard the door open.

"Dan?" someone asked.

I turned around and saw her dad.

"Where's Evie. Where's Emma?" her mom asked.

"Emma is with Alice. I don't know about Evie. No one will tell me anything," I said.

Her dad walked up to the desk.

"My daughter was brought in here. Her name is Evie. Is she okay?" he asked.

"She is doing fine. We got her stitched up and are giving her pain medicine through the IV. We are just waiting for her to wake up," the lady said.

"Can we see her?" her mom asked.

"One at a time," the lady said.

She took us to the room she was in. I looked in and saw her laying on a bed. She was wearing a hospital gown. Her mom walked in first. She only stayed for a few minutes. Her dad didn't want to go in, so he took her mom to the waiting room. I walked in and sat down in the chair beside her bed. I grabbed her hand. I held it up and kissed the top of her hand.

"Come on. You need to wake. Emma needs you. I need you," I said.

I looked up at her face. I saw her eyes start to twitch. It was just a few seconds, and then I saw her pretty green eyes open.

"Dan? What are you doing here?" she asked.

"Alice called me. I had to make sure you were okay," I said.

She nodded her head.

"I'm fine. You should go home and get some rest, you look tired," she said.

I nodded my head and walked out the door. I stopped at the nurses' station and told them she was awake. I went out to my car and drove home.

*****

The next morning, I woke up because I could hear yelling from downstairs. I got up and walked down the steps.

"What are you guys doing here?" I asked.

I saw the boys. They were arguing about something. They usually always are.

"What happened to you last night?" Derrick asked.

"I had to go to the hospital," I told them.

They both gave me a weird look.

"Why? You don't go to the hospital for anything. Ever," Steve said.

"Something happened with Evie yesterday, and I went to go check up on her to see if she was all right," I said.

"Is she all right? What happened?" Steve asked.

"She is better now. She was awake when I left. I'm not one hundred percent for sure what happened other than she got stabbed," I said.

"That's terrible. Doesn't she have an ex-boyfriend or something?" Derrick asked.

"Yeah. So?" Steve asked.

I didn't listen to them. I thought about when I was over at her house. There was a guy there. He was rude to Evie and he hurt Emma. I wonder if he was the guy that Alice saw leave Evie's house. If he was, then that means he is the one that hurt her.

"Derrick, for once you are a genius," I said.

Steve and Derrick both looked at me weird. If there is one thing we can all agree, on it is that Derrick is not the smartest one between the three of us.

Weeks Later

IT'S BEEN SEVERAL WEEKS. I finally got my stitches out. It was nice to not have to worry about tearing them all the time. Tyler has called to come over to see Emma, but I have told him no. Dan has been super nice. He is also very helpful. There are some things that I don't understand, but I guess that happens sometimes. Things just keep getting better. Alice has become a good friend. Haily has been around more. She was helping me with Emma.

"Sweetie, can you come downstairs?" Mom yelled.

"Yes, just give me a second," I yelled.

I put a robe on because I was still in my pajamas, a tank top, and shorts. If Tyler found out, he would be so mad. I walked down the stairs.

"What's up?" I asked.

"Tyler has to come today, but I have to go with your dad. I would have said no, but his lawyer said that if I did say no, we would have to go back to court, but we don't have the money right now," she said.

"It's okay, I will see if Dan or one of his friends can be here with me," I said.

"All right. You go back to get some rest," she said.

I walked back upstairs. None of us have been getting much sleep. We all take turns checking on Emma at night and when she wakes up screaming. I have a doctor's note, so I am good with school until next Monday. It's great that way because I can catch up on sleep and hang out with my baby girl. Dan usually comes over after school. I got my phone and called Dan. He answered after a few rings.

"Hey," he said.

"Hey, I was wondering if either you or one of your friends could hang out with me later because Tyler has to come over to see Emma," I said.

"Yeah, me and Derrick will be there right after school," he said.

"Thank you. I know I put you guys through a lot," I said.

"Don't worry. We want to help keep the two of you safe," he said.

"Okay. I should go. You have to get to school. I will see you later, okay? I love you," I said.

"Love you too," he said.

I hung up the phone. I put my phone on the stand by my bed. I took my robe off and laid down on my bed.

I started to doze off to sleep but was jolted awake when I heard footsteps. I looked around my room and saw Emma walking to my bed.

"I scared, Mommy," she said.

"It's okay, baby," I said.

I moved on my bed to give her room to climb up next to me. Once she was on my bed, I hugged her.

"Baby girl, just to give you a heads-up, your daddy is gonna be coming over later. I know that you are scared to see him, but Dan and his friend Derrick are going to be here to watch over us," I said.

"Okay, Mommy," Emma said.

I laid with her for a while. After a few hours, I gave up on trying to fall asleep. I got up without waking Emma. I didn't want to wake her. She was so peaceful. I went to my closet to change clothes. It was hot out, so I put on shorts and a T-shirt.

I walked downstairs. I made coffee and sat at the table. I was sitting there for a long time when the doorbell rang. I got up and walked to the door. I opened it and saw the boys.

"Hey," I said.

I looked at the clock and saw that it was nearing three o'clock.

"You guys can make yourselves at home. I have to go and wake Emma up before he gets here," I said.

I walked up the stairs. Emma was just sitting up on my bed.

"Hey, baby girl. You need to go get changed, okay? Come downstairs afterward, okay?" I said.

"Okay, Mommy," she said.

I walked back down the steps. I sat on the couch while I waited for Emma to come downstairs. It only took her a few minutes.

When I saw him again, I was sitting next to Dan watching Emma play with Derrick. The doorbell rang. I got up and answered it.

"Hello, Tyler," I said.

"Don't worry, I'm not going to do anything to you. I just want to see my daughter," he said.

I closed the door and we walked into the living room. He saw Emma with Derrick and clenched his fists but didn't say anything. He looked over at Dan too.

"What are they doing here?" Tyler asked.

"They are here to make sure that you don't hurt me again. I mean, you did stab me the last time I saw you," I said.

"Sorry about that," Tyler said.

"It's too late for that. Now I just want to make sure you won't hurt my daughter," I said.

"She's my daughter too," he said.

"Yeah, and she is terrified every time you come around. A daughter is not supposed to feel that way around her father. She is supposed to feel like she is a princess that he adores," I said.

"You're right, and I need to do better and be better for her," he said. "Can you ever forgive me?"

"I will be civil with you for our daughter's sake, but no, I don't think I can forgive you. You just keep doing the same things over and over. You never try to do better," I said.

Emma looked up at me and Tyler from Derrick.

"Mommy, Derrick said something mean," she said.

"I did not. I just said teddy bears are for girls," Derrick said.

"Grandpaw has weedy bears. Is he a girl?" she said.

"Sweetheart, the teddy bears Grandpa has were mine when I was your age." I said.

"He got them now," she said.

I laughed at her. She did have a point there. They might have been mine a long time ago, but he has them now, so they are his.

"I'm telling," she said.

"Emma sweetie, don't you want to talk to your dad before he has to leave?" I asked her.

"No, Mommy," she said.

Tyler looked like he was hurt hearing her say that. I looked a little sad myself. I couldn't imagine hearing my daughter say that about me. I turned and faced Tyler.

"I'm sorry. You can stay and watch her if you want, but I can't force her to talk to you, and I'm not going to make her do anything with you that she doesn't want to," I said.

"It's fine. I'm just gonna go," he said.

I nodded my head and walked with him to the door. He stepped outside.

"Whenever she decides that she wants to talk to me again, can you call me? I would love to see her, but I don't want her to be scared around me anymore," he said.

"Wow, you are different than what you used to be," I said.

"After I hurt you, I had a talk with my mom. She said something that I didn't really think about until now, and it was proven to be true," he said.

"What did she say?" I asked.

"She said that if Emma saw me hurting you, eventually she would be scared of me. It seems like she already is," he said.

"I don't think she is scared of you. I think she is just worried about what you will do," I said.

He nodded his head. He stepped toward me and gave me a hug. I pushed him away very quickly.

"Sorry. Thank you for letting me see her. Do you think I can come back next week?" he said.

"Yes. I will call you and let you know," I said.

"Thank you, Evie." he said.

He turned and walked back to his car. He seemed a little sad. It was strange that he hugged me. Even when we were together, he never really hugged me.

Momma

I WAS SITTING IN THE LIVING room. Emma was up playing in her room. She came down the stairs and sat next to me.

"What's up, baby girl?" I asked.

"Do you tink Daddy is better?" she asked.

"I think he is really trying to be better. He sees that what he was doing was hurting you too, and he wants to be better," I said.

"Can I trust him?" she asked.

"I think we should give him a chance to at least prove that he is trying to get better for you," I said.

She nodded her head and ran back up to her room. I know she misses her dad, but she is afraid that he is going to hurt her. I got up and went to my room. I had to clean my room. I turned on the radio, but I didn't have it up to loud so I could still hear Emma if anything happened. Only a few minutes later, I heard the doorbell ring. I walked out of my room and answered the door. It was Haily.

"Where's my girl at?" she asked.

"She is playing in her room," I said.

Haily squeaked and ran up the stairs. Haily has loved Emma ever since she met her. I thought that it was nice. Emma deserves to have as many people as possible that love her. I went to walk away from the door, but the doorbell rang again. I opened it back up and saw Tyler. He looked at me and gave a small smile.

"I'm sorry I didn't call first," he said.

"It's okay. Come on in," I said.

I opened the door wider and he stepped inside.

"I will go get Emma," I said.

I went to walk away, but he reached out and grabbed my arm. His grip wasn't tight. He immediately let go when I looked at him.

"I actually came to talk to you," he said.

"Okay. Is something wrong?" I asked.

"No, nothing's wrong. My mom has convinced me to get a place in this area so I can see Emma more often," he said.

"Um, I'm not sure about that," I said.

"I will only see her if you are with her. Maybe we can get together after school tomorrow and talk some more about it," he said.

"Sure. That would be great," I said.

"Great. I will see you tomorrow then," he said.

He walked out. I closed the door behind him. Emma came running down the stairs with Haily following behind her.

"Momma, we go for ice cream," she said.

"I'm sorry, honey, but I have work to do here, but Haily can take you," I said.

"Really?" she asked.

"Yeah. You girls have fun. Stay safe," I said.

Emma left the house with Haily laughing. I smiled at them. There was nothing I loved more than hearing Emma laugh. She had such a pretty laugh, and it always made me happy. She was my little princess. I will always protect her and do what I can to make her happy. I went back up to my room to finish cleaning. It took me a few hours.

I went down and sat on the couch once I was done. A few minutes later, Emma and Haily walked in. I looked at them with a smile, but it fell away as soon as I saw Emma. She was crying.

"Baby, what's the matter?" I asked.

"I'm sorry, Evie. I have no idea what happened. On the way back, she fell asleep and when I woke her up, she started crying," Haily said.

I reached out and pulled Emma to me. I picked her up and sat her on my lap. I hugged her.

"It's okay, baby. You are safe. Do you want me to call Grandpa?" I said.

"No, me want Daddy," she said.

"Okay. I can call Daddy if that's what you want," I said.

I got the phone and called Tyler. This is the first time ever that she has asked for him. The phone rang twice, and then he picked up.

"Hello?" he asked.

"Hey, it's Evie. Emma is upset and she asked me to call you," I said.

"Okay. Is it all right if I come over?" he asked.

"Yeah, of course," I said.

"Okay. I will be there soon," he said.

I hung up the phone. I looked at Emma and wiped her cheeks free of tears.

"Daddy said he will be here in a few minutes," I said.

"Okay," she said.

"Why do you want him instead of Grandpa?" I asked.

"Me gots questions," she said.

"Okay. He will be here soon," I said.

I was curious as to what questions she was going to ask. I held her close to me until the doorbell rang. I looked up at Haily. She walked away and answered the door. Tyler walked in with her behind him.

Questions

TYLER LOOKED AT ME AND Emma. Emma looked up at him. He sat down on the couch beside me. I moved my arms so she could get off my lap if she wanted to, but she didn't move.

"I gots questions," she said.

"Okay. Ask away," he said.

I was surprised that he was going to answer them.

"Why hurt Mommy?" she asked.

I looked at her, then to him. I kind of wanted to know the answer to that question myself.

"I hurt your Mommy because I was scared and angry. I didn't realize at the time what I was doing, and how much it was hurting her and you," he said.

"Why do you stab?" she asked.

"I was angry because I thought that she was trying to keep me from seeing you," he said.

"Why hurt me?" she asked.

"I don't know. I honestly don't know. I was mad at your mommy, but I don't know why I hurt you," he said.

"You wove us, right?" she asked.

He looked at me. I nodded my head to tell him to answer. He looked back at Emma.

"Very much, but I don't think your mommy loves me anymore," he said.

She turned and looked at me. I knew what she was gonna ask.

"I used to love your dad very much, but you can only take being hurt so much. He pushed me away and the feelings went away," I said.

She nodded her head at me. I looked over at Tyler. He looked a little sad. I would be too if I just admitted that I still loved him, but he said he didn't love me anymore. I knew what I said probably hurt him, but I want him to know how I feel.

"Are you okay now, baby girl?" I asked.

"Yeah," she said.

I looked over at Tyler. He seemed happy after that. Emma moved off of my lap and got on his. She wrapped her little arms around his neck and hugged him. He put his arms around her tiny waist and hugged her to him. I couldn't help but smile at him.

I watched them for a while and couldn't help the little laugh I gave when Emma started snoring.

"I'll take Emma to bed. You guys can talk," Haily said.

"Thank you, Haily," I said.

Tyler handed Emma over to Haily. Haily walked up the stairs with Emma. I watched them until they got so far up the stairs and I couldn't see them anymore.

"I'm grateful that you called me," Tyler said.

"She wanted me to," I said.

"I know, but after everything I have done, I didn't think you would," he said.

"We should talk about what you said," I said.

"I know you have Dan now. I'm not going to mess that up for you. I want you to be happy. If it means that you are happy with someone else, then okay. I can handle that. I know I never treated you the way that you deserved," he said.

"Thank you," I said.

"Well, I should get back home. I will see you later," he said.

I nodded my head. He walked over to the door and left. I heard his car pull away. I stayed right where I was. Haily came down and sat next to me. We didn't talk about anything. I know she heard what Tyler said, but she also knows I don't feel the same way about him. I checked the time. It was getting late.

"I'm gonna head to bed. You can stay if you want," I said.

"No, it's fine. I'm gonna go home," she said.

I nodded my head. I followed her to the door. I watched her get in her car before I closed the door and locked it. I walked through the downstairs part of the house and turned the lights off. I went upstairs and to my room. I changed into my pajamas and got into bed. I lay on my bed for a few minutes before I fell asleep.

Hiding

A few months later

SEVERAL MONTHS HAD PASSED SINCE Tyler found out that I didn't love him anymore. He said that he was fine with it, but I didn't believe him. He had gone back to acting the way he was before that. He was still being nice to Emma, but when he talked to me, it was different. It felt like the time when I broke up with him after I had Emma. I don't want to see him go back to that. When he is around, I try to hide. Right now, I was hiding. He was there to see Emma, so I was hiding in my room.

My mom was downstairs watching them. I could hear my baby laughing. As long as I didn't hear her cry, I would stay where I was. I only left once my mom said he was gone. I walked down the stairs. Emma was sitting on the floor playing with her toys.

"Why don't you stay down here with them anymore?" my mom asked.

"I feel like Tyler is going back to the way he was. When he talks to me, it sounds like he is dead inside. He was fine a few months ago, but he has slowly been going back to the way he was before," I said.

I didn't know what else to tell her, so I just said the truth. It is good to be honest.

"Maybe you should tell him that. He might not even realize that he is doing that," she said.

"Okay. I will the next time he comes over. I will wait until before he leaves so he won't have to worry about it in front of Emma," I said.

"Does he know that you are with Dan?" she asked.

"Yeah. He said that he was okay with it, but when Emma talks about Dan, I can see that it bothers him. I understand why though. It has to be hard to hear your daughter talk about how great her mom's boyfriend is," I said.

"You would feel the same if the situation was reversed. I know that would kill me if I was in that situation," she said.

My mom did have a point. If it was me in Tyler's shoes and I had to hear how great his girlfriend was, then that would just crush me. I don't even want to imagine how that would feel.

"That would kill me too. I promise I will talk to him the next time before he leaves," I said.

"Good. That's the mature thing to do. Just make sure when you do Dan is not here," she said.

"Okay. I will, Momma," I said.

I walked into the living room with Emma. I sat down on the couch and watched her play with her toys. She had a big smile on her face. She would look up at me once in a while, and I would smile back at her. I love seeing her happy.

When she is happy, you can't help but smile at her. That's just her personality. I hope she never loses that about herself. It is a great quality to have in life. People will want to be around you, but that also means that she will be hurt a lot. I will always be here for her. No matter the situation, I will always be there with her. I'm sure her father will be there for her when she needs him to be. He might not want to be around me, but Emma will always need her father. I can't keep her away from him, and I wouldn't want to as long as she is happy with him being around. If he started to hurt her again, then it would be different, but if he isn't and she is happy with him around, then I wouldn't stop him from coming over.

I was sitting with Emma on the porch. Tyler was supposed to be here again today. I told mom yesterday that the next time I saw Tyler I would talk to him about how I had been feeling.

I know it probably is for no reason, but I just want to make sure that my daughter and myself are safe with him around us.

"Hey, Evie. Are you going to stay with us this time?" Tyler asked.

"Actually, I was wondering if I could talk to you for a few minutes," I said.

"Yeah sure," he said.

We walked into the kitchen. He sat down in one of the chairs. I stood by the counter.

"I don't want to upset you or anything, but I feel like when you talk to me that you are going back to the way you were. When you talk to me, it sounds like you are dead inside and that is what you would always sound like before you would hit me or something. I don't want you to think that you aren't making progress because you are. You are great with Emma, and she loves having you around. I just want you to know that is how I have been feeling the past few times that you have been over," I said.

"I'm sorry about that. My doctor did tell me that I would still have things that I used to do all the time, and I might not notice when I do them. I don't mean to freak you out or anything," he said.

"I thought that might be the case. That's why I decided to tell you about it," I said.

I couldn't tell if he was lying or not. He sounded like he was telling the truth, but with him you never know, and he has been changing for the better. I was watching Tyler play with Emma when a car pulled into the driveway. Dan got out of the car. Emma ran over to him and jumped.

He caught her right away. She was laughing as he walked over to me. I smiled at them. Tyler didn't look too happy, but he didn't say anything.

"Hey," Dan said.

"Hey, I thought you were hanging out with Steve and Derrick today," I said.

"They actually kicked me out of my own house," he said.

I laughed at him. They have done this twice now.

"Why would they do that?" Tyler asked.

"They are planning a party for Haily and using my house. They said I wasn't a good party planner, so I had to leave," Dan said.

I looked over at Tyler and we both laughed.

"I have never heard of someone who was bad at planning parties," Tyler said.

"I don't know. Jake is pretty bad at it too," I said.

Jake is Tyler's friend. They have been friends for a long time. Tyler thought for a second.

"It depends on the party. If it's a party with just his friends, then yeah, but a party where he invites half the town? No," he said.

Jake was always well known around town for his big parties. They were always busted by the cops though, so I guess that was bad. Dan put Emma down. She walked over to Tyler and started pulling him with her.

"Don't get too dirty. Grandma and Grandpa want you to look nice for later!" I yelled.

I turned and looked at Dan. He gave me a questioning look.

"My parents are having some old friends coming over for dinner tonight," I said.

"Oh, that will be fun," he said.

"It will be. Plus, there is going to be a little boy around Emma's age. I hope they get along well enough to play for a few hours," I said.

"Emma is usually very good at listening to you," he said.

I nodded my head. She is really good at it, but there are times where mommy power doesn't work. I smiled and stepped toward him. I gave him a hug. It had been a few days since I had seen him. He needs to come over and hang out with me and Emma more.

"Do you think they will let you back in your house soon?" I asked.

"Probably not. Last time they wouldn't let me back in all night," he said.

"You can stay here until they let you go back home," I said.

"Thank you. That means a lot," he said.

"I'm sure my dad will be happy to see you again," I said.

My dad loves Dan. Ever since Dan helped me the night Tyler threw something through Emma's window, my mom and dad love having him around. They say it makes them feel better knowing that I have someone who will protect me when they aren't at home. I personally don't mind when Dan is here because he makes me feel like I have someone other than my parents, and he makes me feel safe and happy. I know Emma likes him around because she gets a huge smile every time someone talks about him with her around. I know he makes her feel safe, and that is a very good thing with me. It lets me know that she is comfortable with him around.

Date

DAN ASKED ME TO GO on a date with him tonight. Tyler is going to stay with Emma. I'm really nervous about leaving her with him, but my mom said she would stay with them to make sure nothing happens. I know Tyler is getting better, but I still don't trust him completely yet. He could always say that he is getting better when really he isn't. Dan is going to be here in a few hours, so I decided to get ready. I put on a pale pink skirt and a brighter pink top. I grabbed my tan sandals and put them on. I curled my hair and put half of it up in a ponytail. I walked downstairs. Dan should be here any minute.

"You look pretty, Momma.," Emma said.

"Thank you, baby girl," I said.

I looked up at Tyler. He was looking over my outfit.

"You look very nice. He's a lucky guy," he said.

"Thanks," I said.

I walked into the kitchen to find my mom. She looked up at me.

"Aw, sweetheart, you look so beautiful," she said.

"Thanks, Mom," I said.

It was only a few minutes until there was a knock on the door. I heard someone open the door. I got my purse and walked back out to the living room. I hugged Emma.

"You be good, okay? Grandma will make sure you get to bed and have your story," I said.

"Will she tell me the special one?" she asked.

"If you ask nicely, I'm sure she will," I said.

"Okay," she said.

"I will see you later, baby girl. I love you," I said.

"Love you too, Mommy," she said.

She gave me another hug. I got up and walked with Dan out to his car. He opened the door for me and I got in. He closed the door and walked to the driver side. He started driving away from the house.

"So where are we going?" I asked.

"We are going to some place that is peaceful. My mom found it a few years ago when she went on a run. I go there when I want to think," he said.

"So why did you pick there for tonight?" I asked.

"I thought it would be something that you would like. Trust me, when you see it, you will love it," he said.

"Can you see the stars from there?" I asked.

"Yes. They look very beautiful from there too," he said.

I nodded my head. It sounded like it was a very beautiful place. I watched out the window as we drove down the road.

When the car stopped, we were at a parking lot. I looked at Dan.

"Sorry, but we have to walk from here," Dan said.

"Is it worth the walk?" I asked.

"It is definitely worth the walk," he said.

"Okay. Let's start walking," I said.

We walked until we reached a cliff. It was way off of the trail, but I didn't mind. I looked out and could see so many stars.

"Wow, it's so beautiful," I said.

"Yeah, it is," he said.

I looked over at him and saw him staring at me. I couldn't help but smile. I always seemed to smile when he was around. He seemed to know what I liked and how to make me happy. I was never like that with Tyler. Tyler always had to work really hard just to have me give him a fake smile. I always felt afraid with him, but with Dan I feel safe and protected. Things just seem natural instead of being forced.

She's Hurt

IT HAS BEEN A FEW days since my date with Dan. It was really great. I had a lovely time with him. When I got home, Tyler was already gone. I'm just getting ready to leave school. I'm at my locker putting things away. I was still smiling from my talk with Dan. My phone started ringing. I saw that it was Alice.

"I know I'm running late. I'm sorry," I said.

"Evie, it's Emma," she said.

She sounded sad. I paused what I was doing.

"Alice, what's wrong? Is my baby okay?" I asked.

"The ambulance just left with her. I tried to go, but they wouldn't let me. I tried to call your parents, but they didn't answer," she said.

"Okay. Meet me at the hospital," I said.

I hung up the phone. I saw the boys walking over to me with Haily. I started shoving things in my locker as fast as I could.

"Woah, where's the fire, Evie?" Haily asked.

"Emma," I said.

I was close to tears. I saw as her face went from kidding to serious.

"I'm going with you," she said.

I nodded and closed my locker. I walked as fast as I could without bumping into people.

"Hey! Everyone move, now!" Derrick yelled.

Everyone moved to the side and I had a clear path to my car.

"Thanks!" I yelled over my shoulder.

I started running toward my car. I got a text, but I didn't look to see who it was. I got to my car with Haily, and we both got in.

I drove as fast as I could to the hospital. I jumped out before the car could even stop. Haily had to slide into the driver's seat to put it in park. I ran into the hospital. I saw Alice.

"What happened? Where's Emma?" I asked.

"I'm not sure," she said.

I walked up to the counter to the nurse.

"I'm looking for my daughter. Her name is Emma," I said.

"Room 18," she said.

I took off running down the hall. I saw Emma laying on the bed. She looked like she was sleeping. I looked at the doctor standing by her bed.

"Are you the mother?" she asked.

"Yes," I said.

"She's okay now. She is just sleeping," she said.

"What was wrong?" I asked.

"I'm not sure what happened, but she was mumbling about her daddy when she came in and then she had a seizure," she said.

"She's all right now, right?" I asked.

"I hope so. I'm gonna have a nurse take her to the lab for some tests. Please wait in the waiting room, and I will send someone to get you when she's done," she said.

I nodded my head. I leaned over and kissed Emma's forehead.

I walked out to the waiting room. I saw everyone staring at me. I couldn't stop the tears from falling. I got out my phone and called Tyler.

"Hey," he said.

"Where are you?" I asked.

"Woah, why are you mad?" he asked.

"I'm at the hospital with our daughter, and you want to know why I'm mad?" I said.

"Yeah," he said.

"Did you do something to her? I swear, if you did and she tells me when she wakes up, you better hope the cops get you before I do," I said.

I heard a laugh. It fueled my anger even more.

"You're so smart and feisty. It reminds me why I liked you in the first place," he said.

"Did you?" I asked.

"I might have. Did the doctors stop her seizure?" he asked.

"You're a monster. She's only three," I yelled.

"She looked too much like you. I warned you what would happen if you left me," he said.

"I swear, if I find you before the cops-…" I said before he cut me off.

"You'll what? Hurt me? You couldn't even if you tried," he said.

I hung up the phone. My mom looked up at me. I started pacing the floor. I wanted to see my baby.

"What did that monster do?" my mom asked.

Dad looked up at me. I could tell by his look that he was asking if Tyler did do something to her.

I nodded my head to him.

"I don't know. He said that he warned me not to leave him. He even knew that she had a seizure," I said.

"How is he still the same? He was getting notes from doctors and from the court saying that he was doing better," mom said.

"I don't know and I don't care. Right now I just want to know if my baby is all right," I said.

I stayed, pacing the floor until the doctor came out to get me. I walked back with her and sat in a chair next to Emma's bed. I held her little hand up to my cheek.

She's Awake

I STAYED IN THAT CHAIR ALL night long. I didn't want to leave her side. Everyone came in a few times to see her, but then they left. I stayed all night. I never moved from her side. The doctor said that she got the test results back, and it seems that someone gave her some kind of pill or something that caused the seizures, but we won't know who for sure until she wakes up. I watched nurses and doctors come and go all night long. I wanted to help my baby, but I knew the only way I could do that was to let the doctors do their job. It was close to ten o'clock when she finally woke up. I hit the nurse button and stood next to her.

"Mommy," she said.

"It's all right. I'm right here and I'm not going anywhere, I promise," I said.

The nurse walked in and looked over Emma.

"Everything seems to be all right. Can you tell me what happened, Emma?" she asked.

"Daddy gave me candy and told me not to tell Alice or Mommy," Emma said.

"Okay, Emma. The doctor wants to talk to your mommy now, so I am going to sit with you for a few minutes," the nurse said.

"Alwight," Emma said.

"I'll be right back, baby girl," I said.

I walked out and saw the doctor standing by the door.

"Do you have other relatives here that would want to know what's going on?" she asked.

"Yeah. They are in the waiting room," I said.

"Let's go to them and talk," she said.

I nodded my head and followed behind her.

I followed her to the waiting room. I saw my parents and my friends. My dad stood up and hugged me.

"Is there any news?" Haily asked.

"She's awake," I said.

"Unfortunately, I do have some bad news," the doctor said.

"How bad?" I asked.

"Whatever your boyfriend or husband gave her might cause her to have seizures for the rest of her life. We might be able to control them, but we won't know until she has another one," the doctor said.

"What is that going to do with her mind?" Mom asked.

"It will make learning a little harder for her. You will need patience," the doctor said.

"Thank you, doctor," Dad said.

The doctor walked away from us.

"Why would he do this to his own daughter?" Steve asked.

"This is my fault. I should have listened to his warning. I should have known better. I saw the signs that he was still the same, but I didn't do anything," I said.

"This is not your fault, honey. He did this all on his own," Mom said.

"Last night on the phone, he said she looked too much like me, that I should have listened to his warning," I said.

I walked away from them and went to Emma's room. She looked at me when I walked in. I walked over by her bed and sat on the bed beside her. I hugged her.

"I'm sorry, baby. I'm sorry I didn't protect you like I should have. I promise I will do better," I said.

"It's okay, Mommy," she said.

I felt her yawn. I kissed the top of her head.

"Get some sleep, baby. I will stay right here. I won't leave," I said.

It only took her a few minutes before she fell asleep. I stayed next to her and played with her hair. I heard the door open and looked at it. I saw Dan walk in.

"You look very tired," he said.

"I haven't slept in a while," I said.

"I know. You shouldn't blame yourself. You didn't do anything wrong," he said.

"I should have protected her better. I'm her mother," I said.

"There are some things that you just can't control. You get some sleep. I will sit here until you wake up," he said.

I curled my body around Emma. I closed my eyes and thought about what he said. It didn't take long for exhaustion to take over and I fell asleep.

She's Gone

I WOKE UP IN THE HOSPITAL bed alone. I looked but couldn't find Dan or Emma. I was about to start freaking out because she was gone when they walked in.

"You're awake," Dan said with a smile.

Emma came over to me and gave me a big hug. She had a teddy bear in her arms.

"Yeah. I just woke up," I said.

"Sorry if we worried you by not being here," he said.

"Dan bought me a weddy bear," Emma said.

"That's great. You love getting new teddy bears," I said.

Emma crawled over to the bed and sat down. I grabbed the remote for the TV to find cartons.

She ended up watching Mickey Mouse. I leaned back and watched her. Dan was watching the cartoon with her. When Mickey would ask a question, he would give different answers and argue about who was right. It was mainly Dan, but he played it off as if it was her every time. A few times I told her what to say the answer was. She would be right, and Dan would say she cheated. They continued for a few hours before a doctor came in.

"Ms. Mathews, may I speak to you for a moment?" he asked.

"Sure," I said.

I got up and walked out to the hall.

"I know I am not the doctor that you have been seeing the last few days, but I specialize in epilepsy. My name is Dr. Black. Can you tell me more about Emma and her situation?" he said.

"The only thing I really know was that my ex-boyfriend, her father, gave her a pill or something that he told her was candy and not to tell me. I don't really know what happened because I was at school. I was running a few minutes late," I said.

"Who was Emma with?" he asked.

"She was with my neighbor Alice. Alice has been watching Emma for a long time now when I need to be at school and my mom isn't home," I said.

"Do you have a strong bond with your daughter?" he asked.

"I would like to think so. She doesn't get into too much drama yet, but she used to tell me about her nightmares that involved Tyler and the arguments she would get into with my dad about the cartoons they had watched. When I am home, I do as much as I can with her until she falls asleep and then I do my schoolwork," I said.

"Do you know why her father would do this to her? I have a child of my own a few years older than her, and I would never think of hurting him," he said.

"I have no idea why Tyler would do this. I called him when she came to the hospital and that's how I found out that he did something. All I got out of him was that I shouldn't have left him, and she looks too much like me," I said.

"Okay. Thank you for all of that. I am going to be honest with you here. I want her to have another seizure. I don't mean that in a bad way. I want her to have one so I can see her brain waves and find out what kind of medicine she needs that would be best for her to help her. I know this is a difficult question I am about to ask you, but please think about it. I would like your permission to put Emma in a controlled seizure," he said.

"What would that do?" I asked.

"I will be able to see how her brain reacts and be able to understand how to help her better. I would be able to bring her out of it at any time. I just need to see how her brain reacts, and then I will snap her out of it as soon as possible," he said.

"Can I think about it and talk it over with my parents?" I asked.

"Of course. I will be by later and if you haven't come to a decision, then I will see you tomorrow. There is no rush," he said.

"Thank you," I said.

I walked back in the room. Dan looked over at me. He looked concerned. I looked over at Emma and saw that she was fast asleep.

"Anything new?" he asked.

"The doctor wants to put her in a controlled seizure. He said that he will be able to see how her brain reacts and be able to help her better," I said.

"What do you think about that?" he asked.

"I'm not sure. I want him to do whatever he can to help her, but I don't want her to go through all of that again," I said.

"That is understandable. You should talk to your mom about it. She will be able to help you come to a decision better than anyone else," he said.

"Thank you. Not just for this, but for everything you have done since I have met you," I said.

"You don't need to thank me," he said.

He got up and walked out.

After a few minutes, my mom walked in. She gave me a big hug and sat down in the chair Dan had been sitting in. I told her everything the doctor told me and we came to a decision. We waited for the doctor to come back and I told him my decision.

The Test

I WAS OUT IN THE WAITING room. Dr. Black didn't want me back there when he did the test on Emma. I sat out with my parents and waited. It is so difficult to just sit and wait. It kind of reminds me of the time I found out I was pregnant. I had taken the test and the box said to wait three minutes. I was so nervous that all I did those three minutes was pace the floor. I didn't know how I wanted the test to turn out, but I was so happy when I saw that it was positive. I wanted to tell Tyler right away, but he was with his parents, so I had to wait until he came back. When he came back and I told him, he was so happy. It's hard to believe he went from so happy that I was pregnant with her to now purposely hurting her for no reason. I have no idea what goes on in his head to the point where he would even be able to hurt his own child. I would never be able to even think about hurting my baby girl the way he has. Even thinking about not being able to think about it hurts me so much. I wouldn't be able to even try to hurt her. I would do anything to protect her from anyone that I possibly could. I hate knowing there is nothing I can do for her right now. Dr. Black came out and walked to us.

"Is everything all right?" I asked.

"Yes. Emma is back in her room. She is asleep. I do have some good news. I can give Emma something to help her control the seizures, but it won't stop them completely," he said.

"Thank you, doctor," I said.

"You should go be with Emma. I am sure she will want to see you when she wakes," he said.

I nodded and walked off to Emma's room.

I looked at her lying on the bed. She seemed so peaceful. I sat on the chair beside her and just watched her. She looked like she didn't have a care in the world, even after all the things that happened to her. I couldn't help but be so proud of her. All through this, she has been a strong girl. She wasn't very old, but she trusted me enough to know that I would make sure she was all right. Looking at her now I just want her to know that there isn't anything I wouldn't do for her. She is my world and I love her so much. I looked up when I heard the door open. Dan walked in.

"How is she?" he asked.

"She's okay. The doctor said that he could give her medicine that will help control the seizures," I said.

"That's good news," he said.

"Yeah, but the medicine won't stop them completely," I said.

"At least it will be under control. I know it's going to be a lot of work, but don't forget you have your family and friends to help you and you have me," he said.

"Thank you, but I'm not the one that will need the help," I said.

"You won't be able to do this on your own, and we don't want you to. You have so much care and love in you, and we can't just sit back and not help you when you need it. All you have to do is ask one of us to do something and we will do it," he said.

"Thank you. I really appreciate it," I said.

I am glad that I have friends like them. They haven't known me long, but they are all willing to help me when I need it. That is more than what Tyler did. I am still completely shocked by Tyler's turn.

"He wasn't always like this, baby girl," I said to Emma.

Dan sat next to me.

"What was Tyler like before?" he asked.

"Tyler was a really good guy. We dated for a long time. He was my first everything. One time we weren't careful and I was on the pill, but for some reason, it didn't work and I got pregnant, but I'm sure you know how that works. I have no idea how he became like this. He was so happy when I told him. He had just gotten back from a trip with his parents. He came over and told me about it. It was a bad trip that year. His parents split a few months after. I told him once I got home. It cheered him up so much. After I had Emma, he changed. He started thinking that I was going to leave him and take Emma, which eventually I did, but not until my mom caught him one day," I said.

"What did he do?" he asked.

"He was about to hit me. My mom saw and made him leave. After that, we went to court and I got custody of Emma. He could visit, but he had to be supervised. I still have no idea what changed in him to become like that," I said.

"Maybe he was like that all along, and you just couldn't see because of the mask he wore but then it fell off," he said.

"Maybe," I said.

Dan did have a point. Maybe he was like that all along, and I just didn't see it. Maybe I did see it but didn't want it to be true, so I ignored it. I guess love really is blind at times.

Flashback

A few years ago…

I was sitting in my room. Tyler had been with his parents on a trip. I was feeling sick before he left and I went to the doctor. He told me that I had a baby on the way. I could tell that my mom was disappointed in me, but she assured me that she would stick with me through it. We went home and Tyler was on the steps. I ran to him. "What are you doing here? I thought you wouldn't be back until tomorrow," I said.

"I wanted to come home early. I know you weren't feeling well before I left," he said.

"Yeah, I went to the doctor today," I said.

"What did he say?" he asked.

"He said I'm having a baby," I said.

"That's great," he said.

He picked me up and spun me around. When he sat me down, he gave me a kiss. It was so good to have him back at home.

“I’m glad you’re home,” I said.

“Me too,” he said.

He was so happy when I told him about me being pregnant, and now he is the one who is causing our daughter so much pain. I don’t understand how you could do something like this to a child you used to be so happy to have and said you loved with all your heart.

I looked over at Emma in her hospital bed. She had fallen asleep. Dan was still sitting in the chair.

“I can tell that you really loved him,” he said.

“I did. Before all this happened, I was sure that one day would get married, but now all I can think about is how happy I am to not be married to that monster,” I said.

“I guess the world works in messed-up ways,” he said.

I laughed and nodded my head. He was right. The world does work in messed-up ways sometimes. It doesn’t give us choices sometimes. There are times when it just throws things at you and tells you to find a way to deal with it, even if you want a way out of it. Sometimes you just have to find a loophole around what the world threw at you. Tyler became a jerk, but I got to have Emma—and that means the world to me.

Go Home

IT HAS BEEN A FEW weeks since Emma was in her controlled seizure. The doctor is finally letting her go home. Things are finally starting to go back to normal. My dad talked to his boss about help with going to the courts and his boss said he was more than happy to help. My friends have even helped out as much as they could. My dad and I went and talked to the judge while my mom stayed with Emma. The judge took away Tyler's parental rights, so he has no claim to Emma at all anymore. Dan has been amazing through this whole thing. He has come to see Emma every day. He is even the one driving her and me home later today. I am packing everything up for her to take home. She has a few changes of clothes and many new stuffed animals. She is sitting on the bed as I get things together.

"Mommy?" she asked.

"Yes, baby?" I asked.

"Why does Dan love me more than Daddy?" she asked.

I stopped what I was doing. I have no idea how I was supposed to handle this situation. I looked over at her and sat on the bed.

"Is that how you feel?" I asked. "That Dan loves you more."

She nodded. I sighed and watched her. I had no idea what I was supposed to say. I know Dan will be here any minute, so I want to talk to her about it before he gets here.

"I don't know, baby. I guess sometimes people become mommies and daddies and they aren't ready yet," I said.

"Was Daddy not ready?" she asked.

"I think your daddy has some other problems that he needs to deal with before he can be ready to be a daddy. Maybe sometime in the future, he will try to make things better with you, but I don't think he will be ready for a very long time," I said.

"Did Daddy make me sick on porpose?" she asked.

"It's purpose, baby," I said. "I don't know. That is something you would have to ask him." I didn't like lying to her, but that is not something she needs to know at this young of an age.

There was a knock on the door and I looked over. Dan was standing there. I looked back at Emma and she had the biggest smile.

"Are you girls ready to go home?" he asked.

"Ya!" Emma cheered.

I laughed a little. She jumped off the bed and ran toward Dan. He caught her easily. I grabbed her bag and walked next to him. He put her down and she started walking in front of us. He grabbed my hand as we were walking.

"What was with that conversation back there?" he asked.

"She asked why you love her more than Tyler," I said.

He looked over at me. I glanced at him before looking back to Emma. He looked a little shocked about what I said.

"She feels that way about me?" he asked.

"She said she does," I said. "I can see why she would feel that way though. You have been with her every day since she came to the hospital. Tyler is the reason she was here in the first place."

He hummed like he was thinking about it.

"I guess that does make sense," he said.

We followed behind Emma as she was skipping through the halls. It was so good to see her acting like her normal self again.

We pulled into the driveway of the house. I got out and got Emma out of the car. She ran up to the door to go inside. My parents were there waiting for her. I grabbed her stuff from the back seat. Dan walked over and stood next to me. I closed the car door and looked to where Emma and my parents were.

"She is an amazing little girl," he said.

"She is," I said.

I couldn't help but smile. My little girl is so strong for going through everything that Tyler has put her through.

"I thought about what you told me back at the hospital," he said.

'Yeah?" I asked.

"Yeah," he said. "I do love her. Just about as much as I love you."

I looked over at him and smiled. I stood up on my toes and kissed him. He started to deepen the kiss, but Emma yelled for us to hurry up. I pulled away from him and we both laughed. We started walking toward the house.

Life may have thrown us some curveballs, and we might not know what is going to happen in the future, but for the moment things are absolutely perfect, and I wouldn't want to change anything.

To be continued...

About the Author

KIMBERLY HAS ALWAYS USED WRITING as an escape. When she had a bad day she created a happy ending in a story. Writing became something that Kimberly made sure to do every day. Writing became one of Kimberly's biggest passions that she loves doing all the time.

CPSIA information can be obtained
at www.ICGtesting.com
Printed in the USA
LVHW091957010821
694269LV00004B/661